BABAYAN AND THE MAGIC STAR

Kiku Adatto was born in Yokohama, Japan, and grew up in the United States and Europe with her parents, brother and sisters. Every night her father, an immigrant from Turkey, told stories that blended East and West. She continued this tradition, and *Babayan and the Magic Star* grew out of the bedtime stories she told her two sons when they were young. With *Babayan and the Magic Star* she seeks to revive the oral storytelling tradition by encouraging children to interpret, retell and continue the story in their own voice and adapt it to their local cultures and traditions. She hopes to inspire children to see storytelling as part of discovering and transforming the world.

An award-winning teacher at Harvard University, Kiku is a noted author, scholar and commentator on art, popular culture and civic life. She is married to political philosopher Michael Sandel.

Roger Bowman is a distinguished painter and printmaker. His art has been exhibited in galleries and museums throughout the United States. His paintings are known for their vibrant colours and striking visual poetry. These are qualities he brings to the illustrations for *Babayan and the Magic Star*, which is his first children's book. Born in Jonesboro, Arkansas, Roger is currently Professor of Art at the University of Central Arkansas in Conway, where he lives with his wife, Jima.

BABAYAN
and the Magic Star

KIKU ADATTO

Illustrated by

ROGER BOWMAN

RED TURTLE
RUPA

Published in Red Turtle by
Rupa Publications India Pvt. Ltd 2014
7/16, Ansari Road, Daryaganj
New Delhi 110002

Sales centres:
Allahabad Bengaluru Chennai
Hyderabad Jaipur Kathmandu
Kolkata Mumbai

Copyright © Kiku Adatto 2014
Illustrations copyright © Pucker Art Publications 2014

This is a work of fiction. Names, characters, places and incidents are either the product of the author's imagination or are used fictitiously, and any resemblance to any actual persons, living or dead, events or locales is entirely coincidental.

All rights reserved.
No part of this publication may be reproduced, transmitted, or stored in a retrieval system, in any form or by any means, electronic, mechanical, photocopying, recording or otherwise, without the prior permission of the publisher.

ISBN: 978-81-291-2995-6

First impression 2014

10 9 8 7 6 5 4 3 2 1

The moral right of the author has been asserted.

For sale in the Indian subcontinent only

Printed at Replika Press Pvt. Ltd., India

This book is sold subject to the condition that it shall not, by way of trade or otherwise, be lent, resold, hired out, or otherwise circulated, without the publisher's prior consent, in any form of binding or cover other than that in which it is published.

Contents

Babayan	1
The Magic Star	3
Shayma Bayma Island	5
The Great Debate	7
The Book of Names	13
First Night	16
Kookatu, Teema and Paw	19
The Talking Palms	24
The Attack of the Kura Birds	29
The Migrating Swans	35
The Voyage	37
The Faraway Islands	43
A Joyful Roar	48

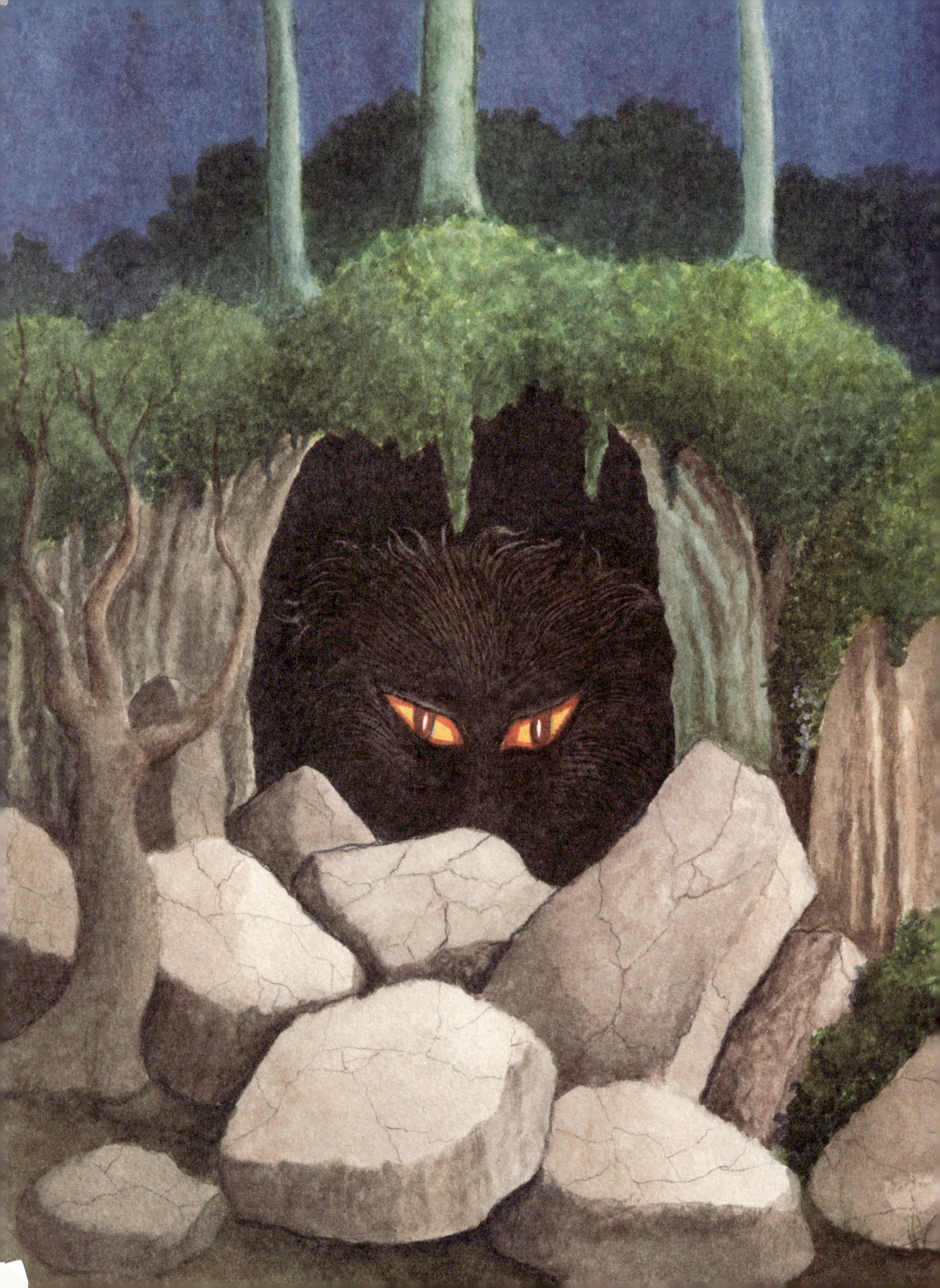

Babayan

Many fierce monsters have roamed the hills and valleys of the far north, but none as fierce as Babayan. Babayan lived in a cold, dark cave, and his heart was as cold and dark as the cave he lived in. He was known for his mighty roar and wild hunger. Babayan would swoop down from his cave and eat everything in sight: cows, sheep and horses for dinner and huts and haystacks for dessert. When he was full, it was quiet. When he was hungry, the ground shook.

All the villagers feared Babayan. They feared him when they plowed their fields, drew water from their wells and when they went to bed at night. 'Will Babayan always be with us?' the children asked. 'Babayan is like the ice, the storm and the avalanche,' their parents answered. 'He will always be with us. Sleep well and be glad he doesn't eat people.'

And so life went on until one summer evening. The dark shadow of Babayan fell across the valley. The shepherds fell to the ground. Babayan rushed down upon the sheep. Suddenly, there was a burst of light, and Babayan disappeared.

The villagers waited and waited for Babayan to return, but he never did, so they rejoiced in their quiet life and thought of Babayan no more. They never thought to wonder, 'What happened to that wild monster when he disappeared from the hills on a summer's evening?'

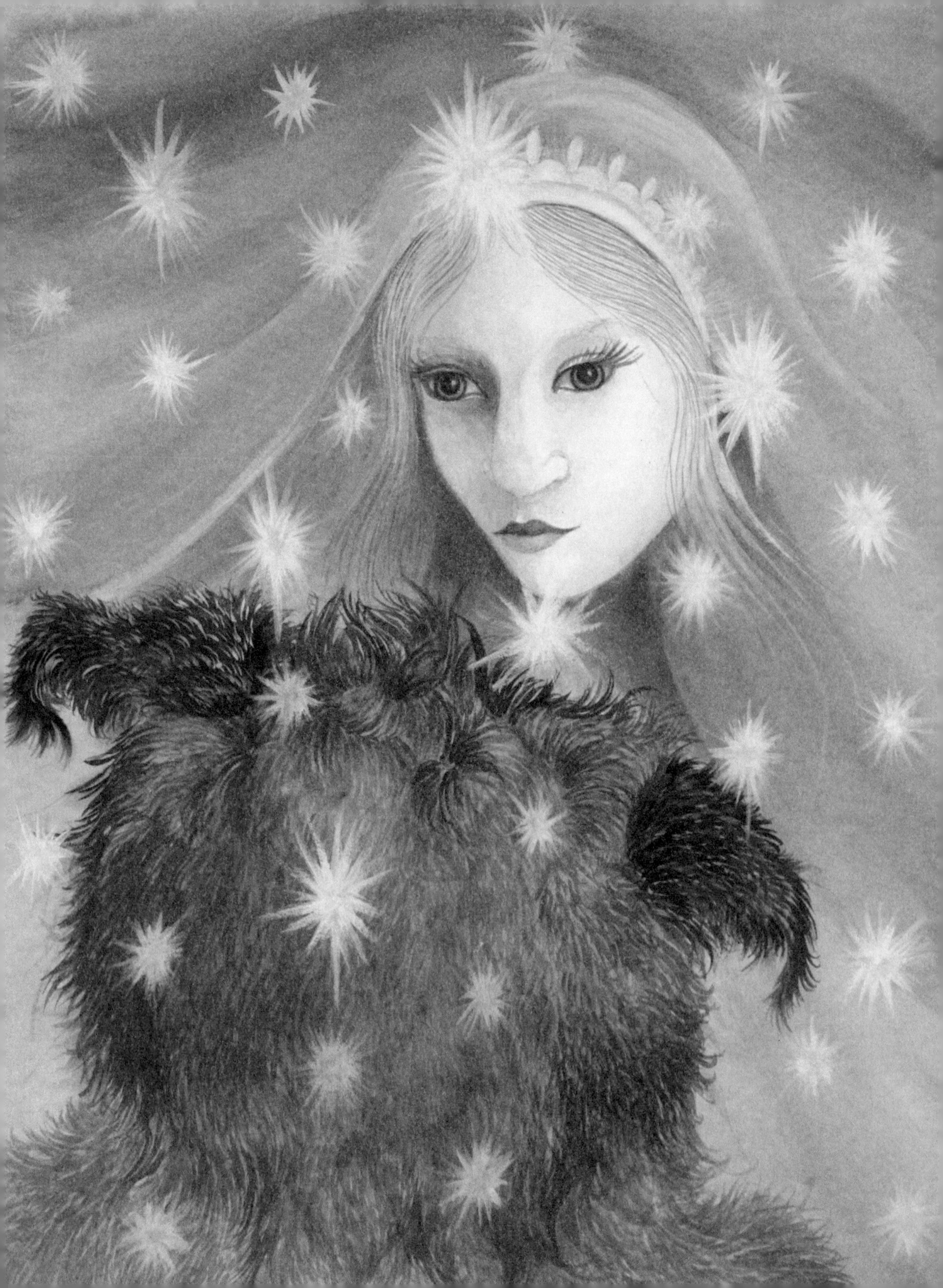

The Magic Star

Babayan was flying through the sky and he did not know why. He shot through a cloud, tumbling further and further into the blue-black night. He might have tumbled forever, but he reached for the edge of a star. And there he dangled. It was cold, dark and still. The earth was far away.

Babayan roared his mighty roar, but the roar only echoed in the night. 'I am all alone,' thought Babayan. 'And I am afraid of my own voice.'

Hours passed. Or it could have been days. And still Babayan dangled.

Then, from the stillness, a voice called, 'Babayan. Babayan.'

'Here I am.'

'Are you the great monster who is bigger than a house, who can swallow a sheep in one bite, whose roar can knock down ten men?'

'Yes, I am the one. But now I am alone.'

The Queen of the Stars appeared in a burst of silver light.

'I will help you return to earth, but you will not be the same.'

'Who will I be?' asked Babayan.

'You will discover.'

The Queen of the Stars walked away on a stairway of silver stars.

'Wait. Wait,' called Babayan.

'If you are in danger, I will come,' answered the Queen of the Stars. Then she disappeared. Babayan's eyes closed. He fell slowly back to earth.

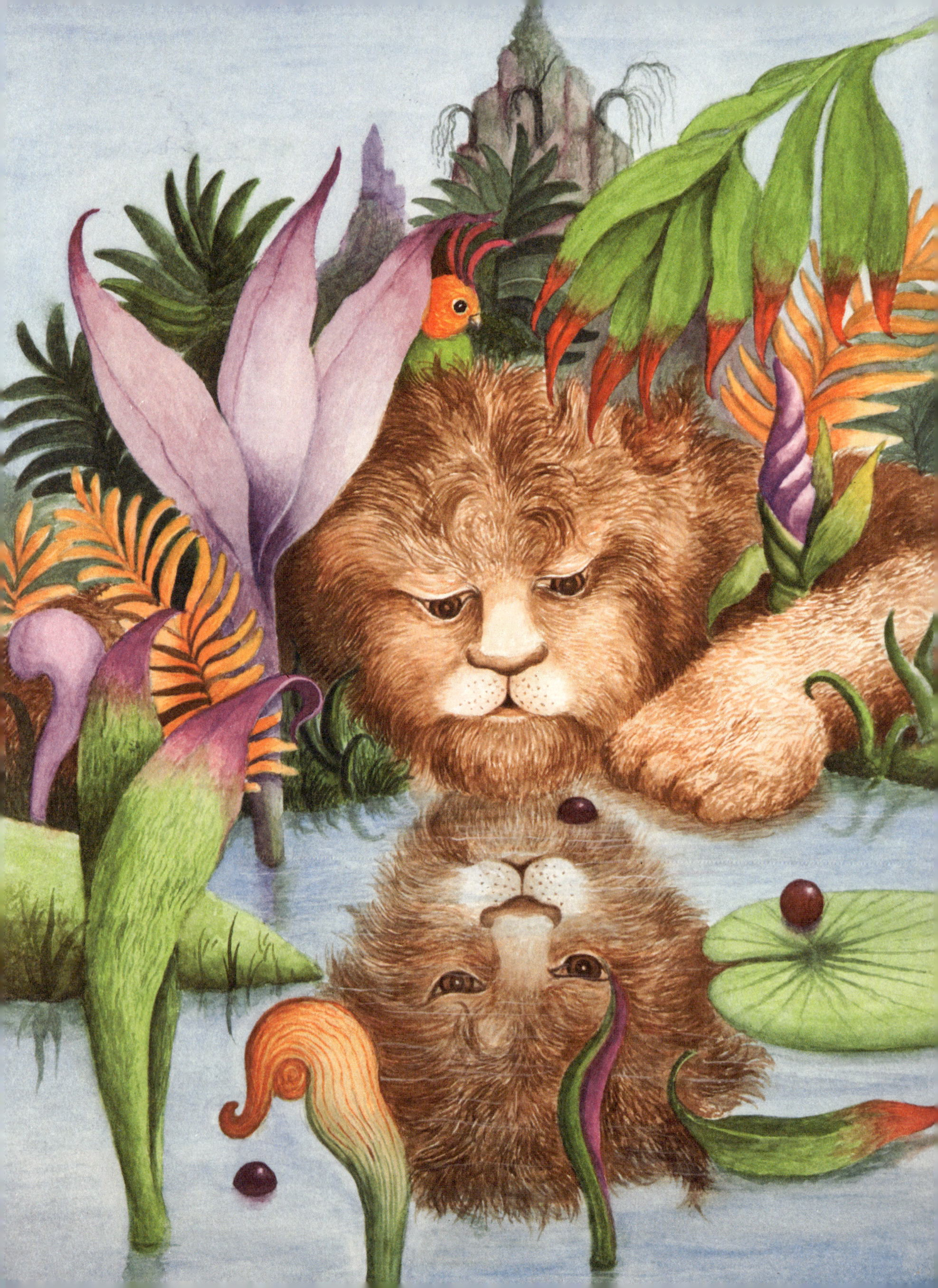

Shayma Bayma Island

As Babayan tumbled back to earth, his angry face grew calm, his rough fur fell away, and he grew a new and lighter coat. He had shot up in the sky from the hills of the far north and now he was falling to the other side of the world, past the equator, through the clouds, down to the South Seas, to a place no map named: the hundred-island kingdom of Shayma Bayma.

When Babayan woke up, he did not know where he was. Even though it had been a long time since he had eaten, he was not hungry. The sun was warm on his fur, and he drank in the greenness of the forest. Frilled lizards chased each other around his legs, ants scurried up a tulip tree and hummingbirds flapped their iridescent wings among the flowers.

Babayan stood up and stretched his arms and legs. His muscles felt strong, but he had no idea how big and strong he really was.

The ants, birds and plants were much larger than any he had seen in the hills of the north. 'Have I gotten smaller?' wondered Babayan. 'Or does everything grow bigger here?'

Babayan had never looked at himself before, but now he was curious. He found a pool in a clearing by the sea, but just as he looked down into the water, he was startled by the frightened cry of birds. 'Hurry, hurry to the hiding cave,' they called. 'The sea dragons are coming!' Many animals rushed by him in a blur of frightened eyes and feet.

Babayan heard great roars coming from the sea. Fire leapt over the waves. The water churned with the beating of the dragons' wings. The dragons drew closer and closer. Their red eyes glowed as they charged through the sea. Babayan ran to the water's edge. He roared his mighty roar. A great wave rose up and chased the sea dragons away.

'My roar is more powerful than ever,' thought Babayan. Then he sat down to eat bananas and mangoes in the warm sun.

The Great Debate

Back in the hiding cave, a great debate was taking place about Babayan. 'The sea dragons are gone, but we are in another fix,' said the mother parrot. 'That beast is as tall as a young palm. My ears are still ringing from his roar.'

'The question is,' said Grandfather Monkey. 'Is he friend or foe?'

'Friend,' argued one of the coral apes. 'In fact, I think he's a relative. One of my cousins on Coconut Island had an unusually large baby some years back, and that's probably him all grown up.'

'Nonsense,' argued one of the sea bears. 'He's no more an ape than my Uncle

Jobo. He's a giant white bear who washed in from the lands of the far north. He couldn't take the sun and now his fur has turned brown.'

'You're both wrong,' said the salamander with a satisfied smile. 'He's not a bear

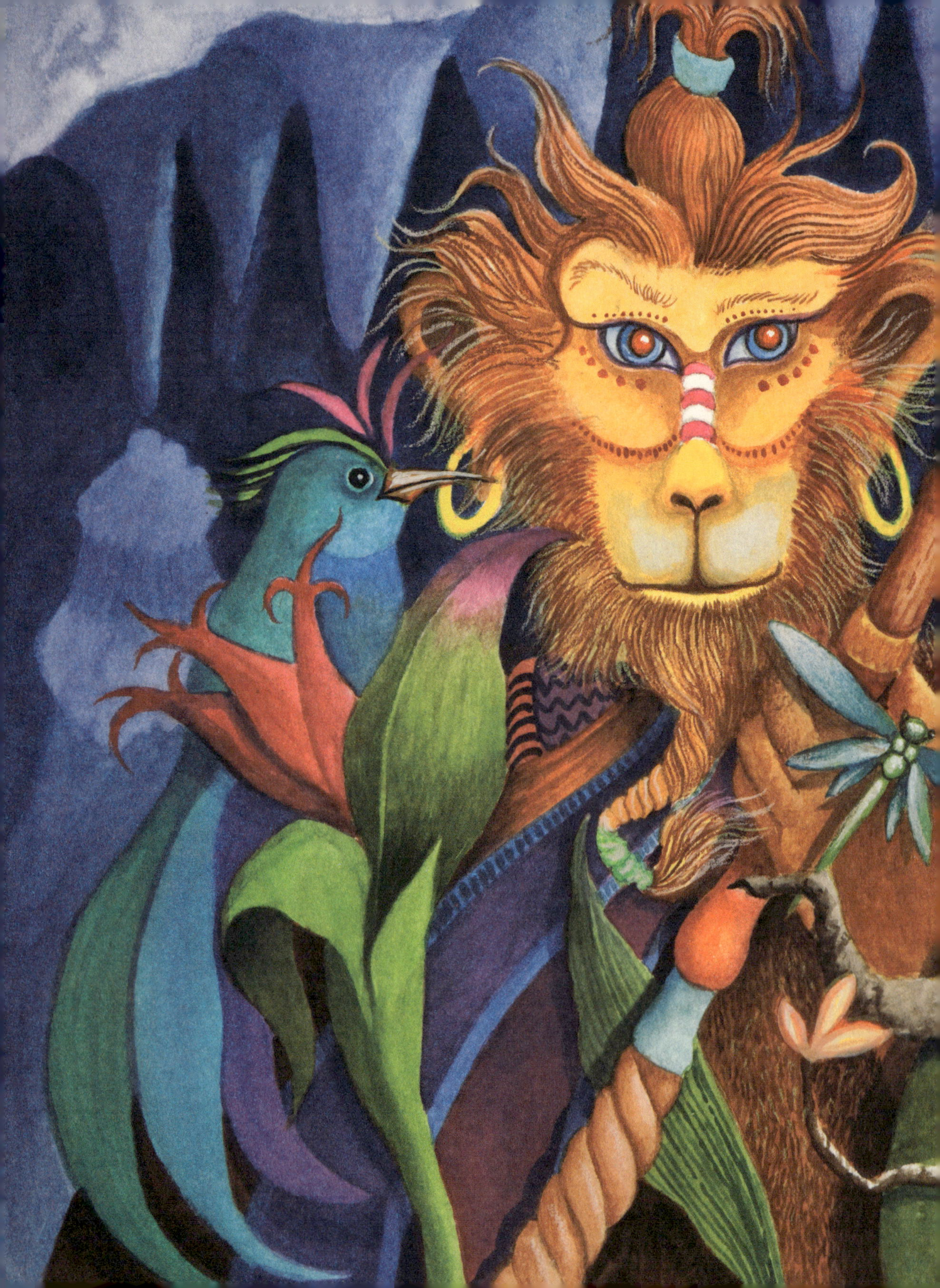

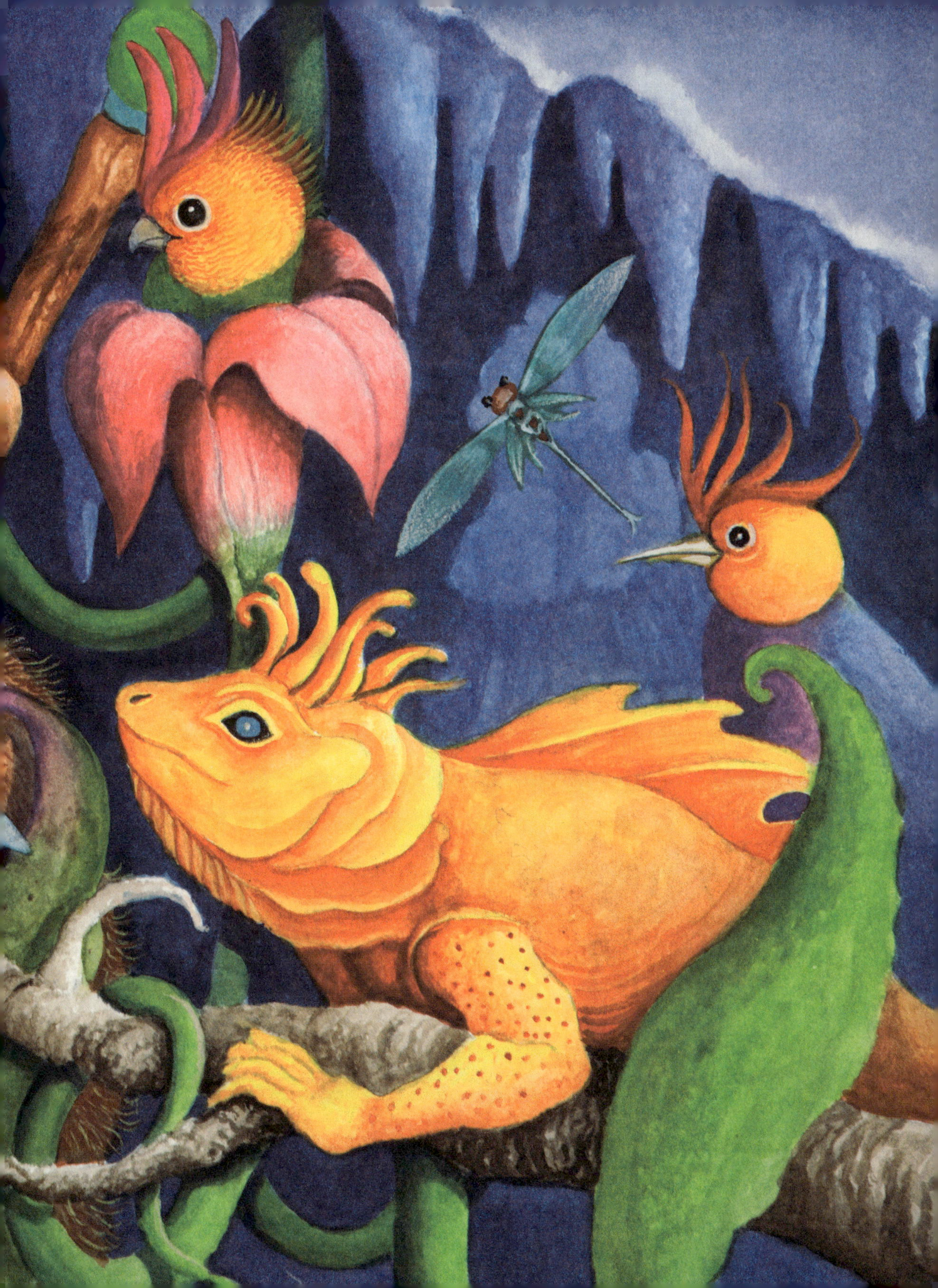

or an ape, but a monster with a head bigger than the moon. And that information comes from the best authority: the fish who saw him looking into the pool.'

'We all have our theories,' said Grandfather Monkey. 'But the time has come for a volunteer to go out and have a closer look.'

'Me, me, me!' chirped the young parrot Kookatu.

Kookatu's parents stepped forward. 'Our son is too young for such a dangerous mission. We will go. Kookatu, you stay here and help guard the cave.'

The cave door was opened a crack and the mother and father parrot flew out, and before anyone could stop him, Kookatu squeezed through the opening and flew after his parents.

The Book of Names

From a perch in a breadfruit tree, the mother and father parrot watched Babayan sitting by a pile of broken coconuts and half-eaten bananas.

'He seems to like fruit, but what if he also likes parrots and monkeys and pumas?' worried the father parrot.

'He has kind eyes,' observed the mother parrot. 'But his claws are sharp.'

While his parents were talking, Kookatu hopped up to Babayan and asked, 'Do you plan to eat me?'

'No,' said Babayan. And with a smile and glance towards the breadfruit tree, he added, 'I would not even consider a monkey or a puma.'

'Hooray!' chirped Kookatu. He flew up to Babayan's head and ran around his furry ears.

'I guess that settles it,' sighed the mother parrot, as she watched Kookatu hanging upside down from one of Babayan's fingers. 'Go send word to the others. The beast is friendly.'

The animals made a circle around Babayan. The elders of the island came forward. 'We are among the lost islands of the earth,' said Grandfather Monkey. 'A great and ancient magic protects us. We are invisible to men.'

'That is good,' said Babayan. He could not remember why, but the thought of men made him feel uneasy.

'Life is peaceful here,' continued Grandfather Monkey. 'Though we do have

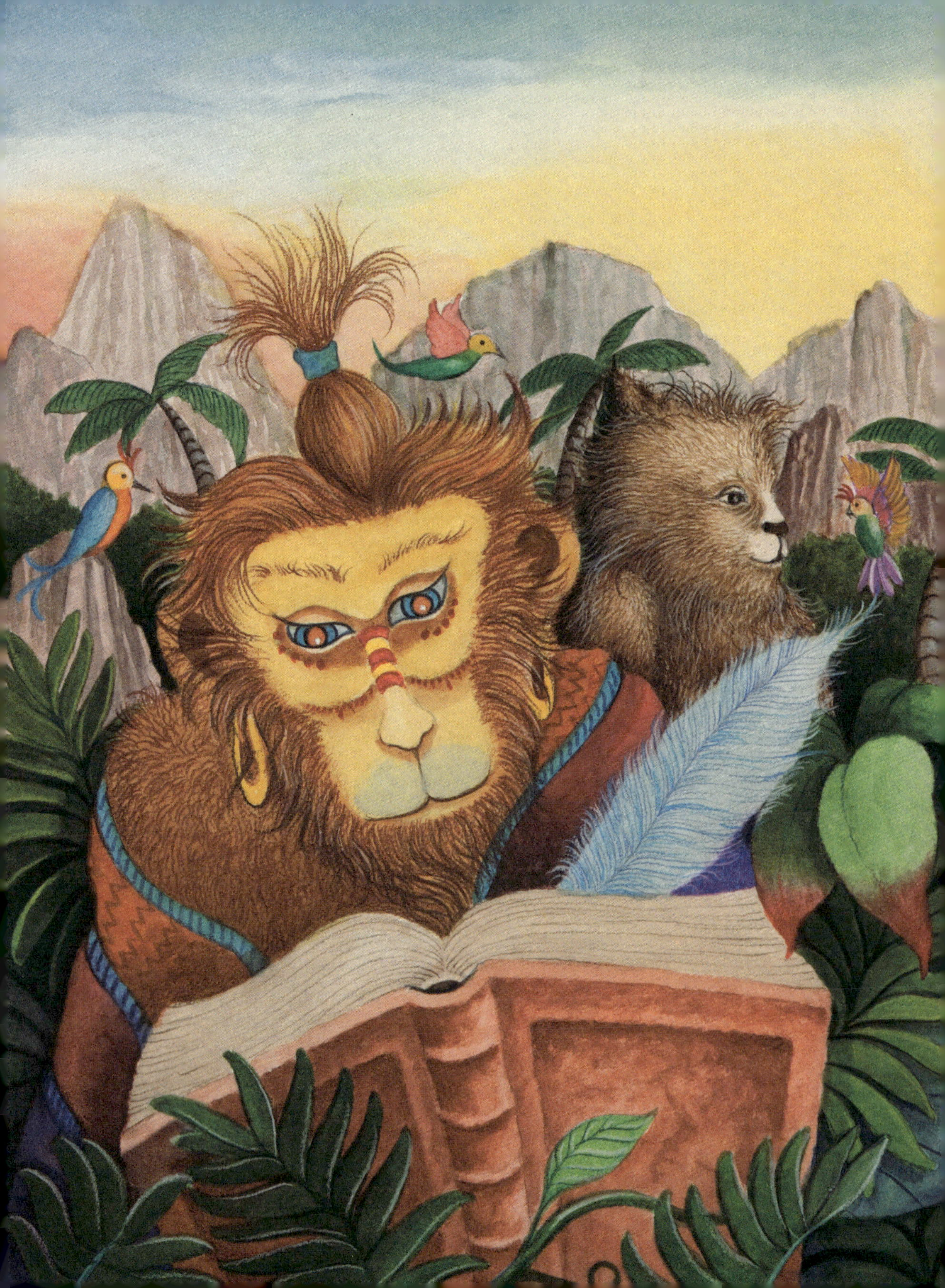

problems with invaders from time to time. Those sea dragons were a regular nuisance until you came along.'

'Thank you,' said Babayan, with a shy nod of his head.

'May I ask your name and where you are from?' enquired Grandfather Monkey.

'I am Babayan. I fell from a star.'

'Then you are welcome,' said Grandfather Monkey. 'Welcome to Shayma Bayma.'

The young animals gathered around Babayan. Grandfather Monkey walked off by himself. He opened the Book of Names and began to turn the pages. In it was recorded how each creature came to the hundred-island kingdom of Shayma Bayma. He came to the page, 'Fell from a Star', and wrote 'Babayan.'

First Night

The excitement of so many changes in such a short time suddenly made Babayan feel sleepy.

'Where can I find a comfortable cave where I can take a long nap?' he asked.

'Caves aren't for sleeping,' laughed Kookatu. 'Sleep under the stars and learn their stories.'

Kookatu helped Babayan choose a spot in a clearing not far from the flowering

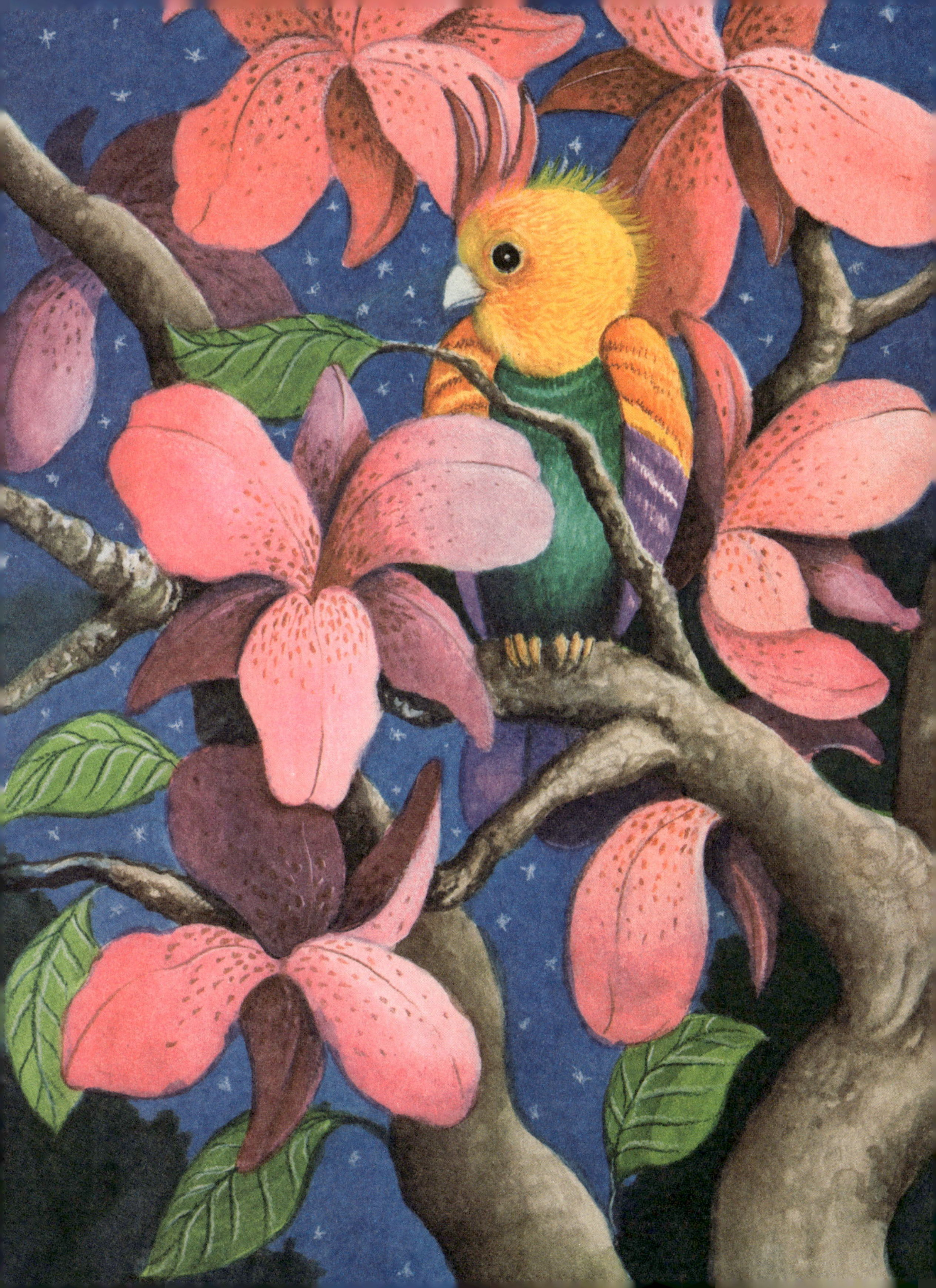

orchid tree where the parrot family lived. The coral apes and sea bears, who felt a special kinship with Babayan, made him a soft bed of leaves and vines.

Babayan lay down in his bed and looked up at the evening stars. He had forgotten his old life. He only remembered dangling from a star and his meeting with the Queen of the Stars.

'Thank you for sending me to Shayma Bayma,' he said quietly.

From high in the flowering orchid tree a little voice echoed, 'I asked you to send me a friend. Thank you for sending me such a big one.'

Babayan yawned a big yawn and Kookatu yawned a little yawn. The stars twinkled like the eyes of the Queen of the Stars, and Babayan and Kookatu fell asleep.

Kookatu, Teema and Paw

'Wake up,' chirped Kookatu as he shook the water from his wings over Babayan's face. 'That's your morning shower.'

'But it's still dark, and I'm still dreaming.'

'We must begin our journey before the morning light. I've decided to give you the grand tour.'

Shayma Bayma Island was covered in mist. The sea breeze carried the memory of night as Babayan followed Kookatu past the surrounding islands. Many of the creatures that slept in the darkness were unknown to Babayan, for the Shayma Bayma Islands were lost in a time when the earth was still new. Kookatu rode on Babayan's shoulder as they waded past the islands of the great horned zebrons, the golden kangaroos and the flying turtles.

'Many animals in our kingdom have their own island; even some of the rocks and trees do,' chirped Kookatu.

The mist was lifting when they came to Big Cat Island. The lions, tigers, leopards and pumas were sprawled out on the ground and in the trees, fast asleep. Sometimes their wide mouths opened as they snored and their sharp teeth glistened. Kookatu darted from one to the other looking into each sleeping face.

'Aren't you afraid you might get eaten?' asked Babayan.

'No. We have a "no eating" rule here. We've given up on the idea of predator and prey. It created a lot of hard feelings.'

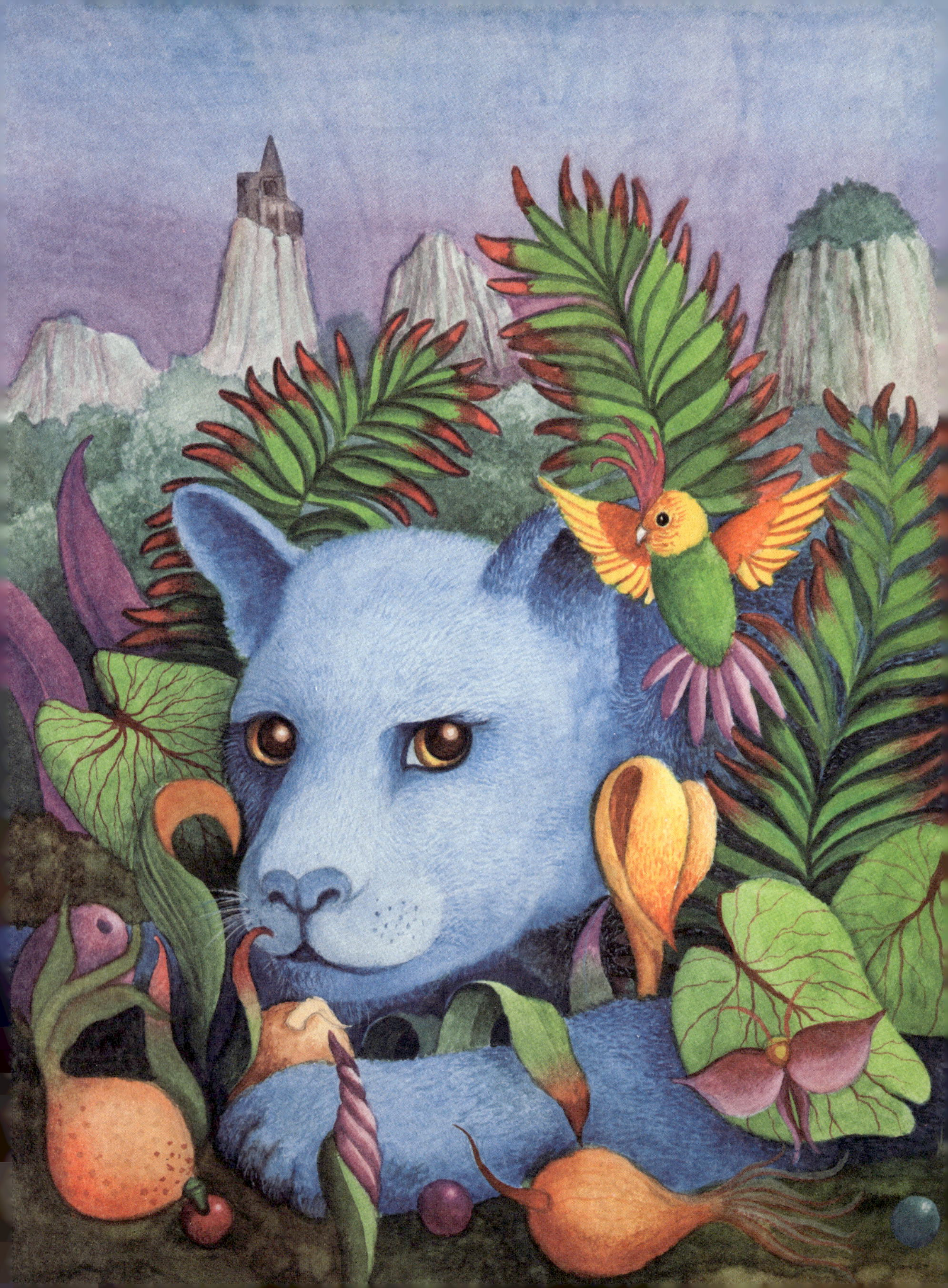

Kookatu found his friend, Paw, a twilight-blue puma, and woke him up with a soft whistle. 'Meet my friend, Babayan,' whispered Kookatu. 'He dropped from the sky yesterday.'

'Oh, he's wonderfully grand,' thought Paw as he walked by Babayan's side.

The tide was low and the sun was rising when they waded towards Monkey Island. Teema, the tea monkey, was waiting on a rock far out on Monkey Bay. He had met Babayan the day before and greeted him with his best double flip. 'Jump up on my shoulder,' laughed Babayan.

They went north to the Island of the Shining Pools and took a shower under the Shining Falls. Then they travelled west for a leisurely breakfast on the Island of a Hundred Fruits. They hiked through Song Bird Island and began to pass the Tea and Cocoa Islands when Teema's nose began to twitch. 'The winds are beginning to shift. Remember Grandfather Monkey's warning. This is when the creatures from the Wild Islands stir.'

Babayan wanted to ask about the Wild Islands, but the shifting winds made his shoulders tremble and his stomach whirl. He felt an urge to run and roar. The Wild Islands seemed to be calling to him, and the voices of his friends were far away. Only Kookatu noticed the distant look in Babayan's eyes and saw how the fur on his body began to rise.

Up ahead, Paw and Teema were splashing through the warm, shallow waters of the Shayma Bayma Sea. 'Grandfather Monkey is such a worrywart,' Paw reassured Teema. 'Who cares what the winds do? We are safe with Babayan.'

'You're right,' nodded Teema. He jumped on Paw's back and whispered in his ear, 'Should we tell Babayan about our hidden treasure?'

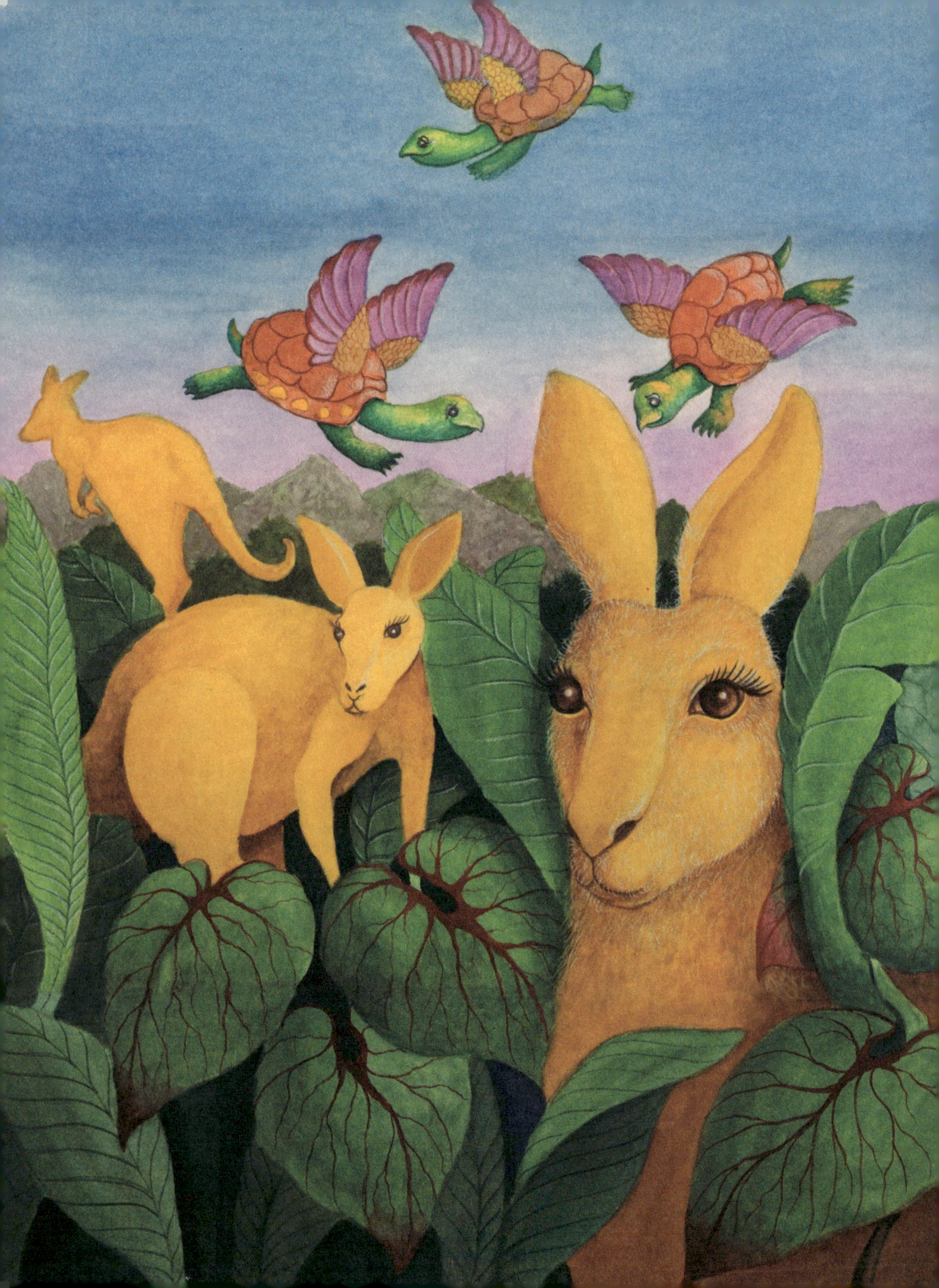

'No,' answered Paw. 'Let's wait until we get to Palm Island.'

As they approached Palm Island, a gentle light returned to Babayan's eyes. Kookatu saw the light and soared above Babayan's head. When he landed on Babayan's shoulder, the trembling had disappeared.

The Talking Palms

Palm Island was lush and cool and green. It had the best coconuts, but a bad reputation. That was because every time you picked a coconut, another coconut would hit you on the head. No one ever bothered going there except Kookatu, Teema and Paw.

And that was just the way the Palms liked it. From the shore, three of the grandest Palms saw Babayan and his friends coming.

'I spent all morning arranging my fronds and now this had to happen.'

'Now dear, that parrot, monkey and puma have never been a problem.'

'But look what they have brought with them. If that creature ruffles my fronds, I'll scream.'

'Pull yourself together! They are so close now they might hear us, and our secret will be out.'

When Babayan, Kookatu, Teema and Paw walked on to the beach, all was quiet. Babayan's head bobbed up and down among the treetops as they walked deeper and deeper into the grove of Palms. Sometimes, Babayan thought he heard whispering voices. Once, when he brushed too close to a palm tree, he was slapped in the face by a frond.

The sun was high in the sky when they came to the Silver Falls.

'Behind the falls is a hidden cavern,' called Kookatu, as he and Teema darted behind the glistening water.

Babayan edged along the steep wall of rocks by the falls and crawled behind Paw until they came to a large cavern. There, in the darkness, was a clay pot filled with shimmering stones.

'We collected these from all the Shayma Bayma islands,' Teema said with pride.

'Choose one,' chirped Kookatu.

Babayan chose a white stone that was hidden among the rest. It was smooth and cool, but as he held it in his paw, it grew warm and glowed, shooting hundreds of tiny stars on the ceiling of the cavern. Then the light withdrew into the stone.

'A Star Stone,' exclaimed Paw. 'When our island kingdom was formed, the Queen of the Stars scattered a handful of stones over it.'

'They have a powerful magic,' added Teema. 'Only a few have been found. And that was a long time ago. The elders have guarded them for generations.'

'And they don't let anyone touch them,' whispered Kookatu, as he brushed his wing over the Star Stone and touched it solemnly with his beak.

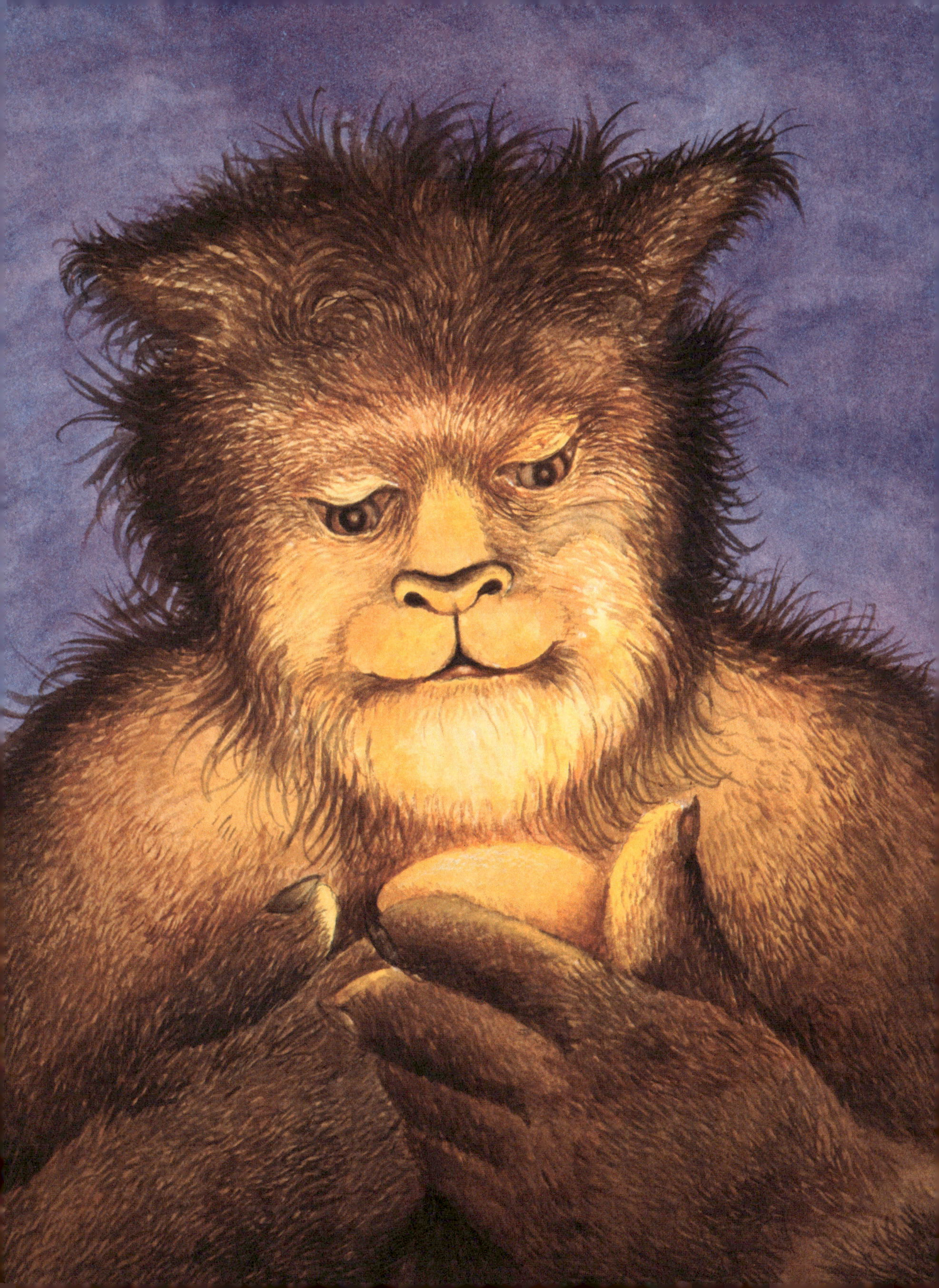

'Let's bring it home and show Grandfather Monkey,' suggested Teema.

'But how will we keep it safe?' worried Paw.

'I have an idea,' said Kookatu. 'Let's make a necklace of seaweed and vines and put the stone around Babayan's neck.' When they were done, Babayan bowed his head and thanked his friends. The Star Stone rested quietly on his mighty chest.

The Attack of the Kura Birds

Babayan, Kookatu, Teema and Paw went out of the cavern to have their midday meal. The warm sun and the sound of the falls made everyone sleepy. Kookatu flew up to a blue willow tree and tucked his head under his wing. The others rested by the falls and watched the clouds flying over the forest.

Suddenly, a dark shadow fell over the Palms. Giant Kura birds circled high above the clearing. Their great ebony wings glistened and their beaks shone like flashing swords. Kookatu, Teema and Paw ran behind the falls. Babayan stood alone. He roared his mighty roar, but the Kura birds were used to the roar of volcanoes, and they were not afraid.

With piercing screeches, they swooped down and attacked Babayan from every side. Babayan twirled and swatted the Kuras with his mighty paws. Still the Kuras attacked, but with each attack, the Star Stone burned brighter, and Babayan's strength increased.

As the leader of the Kuras swooped over him, Babayan grabbed him by his feet, swung him over his head, and flung him far out to sea. There was a moment of silence, then a great splash. The rest of the Kura birds fled in terror.

'You fought well, beast,' came a voice from the treetops.

'Who's there?' asked Babayan.

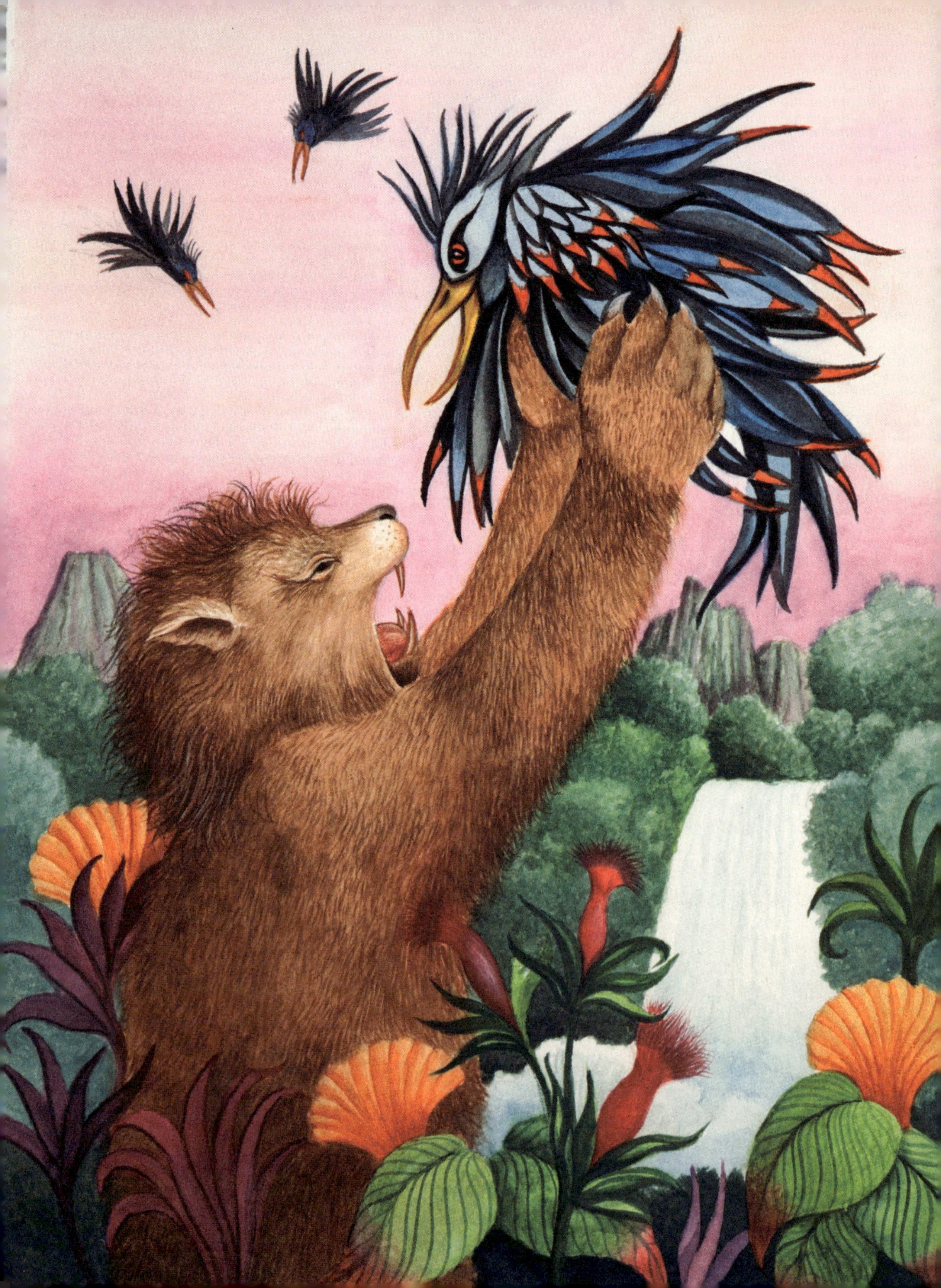

'If you would kindly introduce yourself, we'll tell you.'

'I am Babayan.'

'We are the Palms. We do not like intruders, and frankly, those nasty birds were the ultimate. It will take us days to put ourselves back together again.'

'Why did they attack me?' asked Babayan as he brushed some giant feathers off his bruised arms.

'You looked delicious. That's why,' answered one of the Palms.

'Yes, dear,' added another Palm, as she leaned over to take a closer look at Babayan. 'Why should they spend all day eating snacks when they can have a lovely dinner in one fell swoop? The creatures from the Wild Islands think only of their stomachs.'

'I never thought of myself as someone's dinner,' said Babayan.

'Well, we are not all fortunate enough to be born a Palm. But enough small talk. Thank you, dear beast. You are welcome among us as long as you promise never to tell anyone we can talk.'

'I will keep your secret,' whispered Babayan as he gently rearranged some of their bent fronds.

Kookatu, Teema and Paw peeked out from behind the Silver Falls.

'It is safe,' Babayan called to his friends. 'And now we must go.'

When they returned to Shayma Bayma, Grandfather Monkey was waiting for them. He saw the Star Stone resting on Babayan's chest, and sent Kookatu, Teema and Paw home to their families. He took Babayan to his hut and gently rubbed soothing herbs on his wounds.

'I felt the Wild Islands calling to me,' Babayan murmured in a voice hoarse

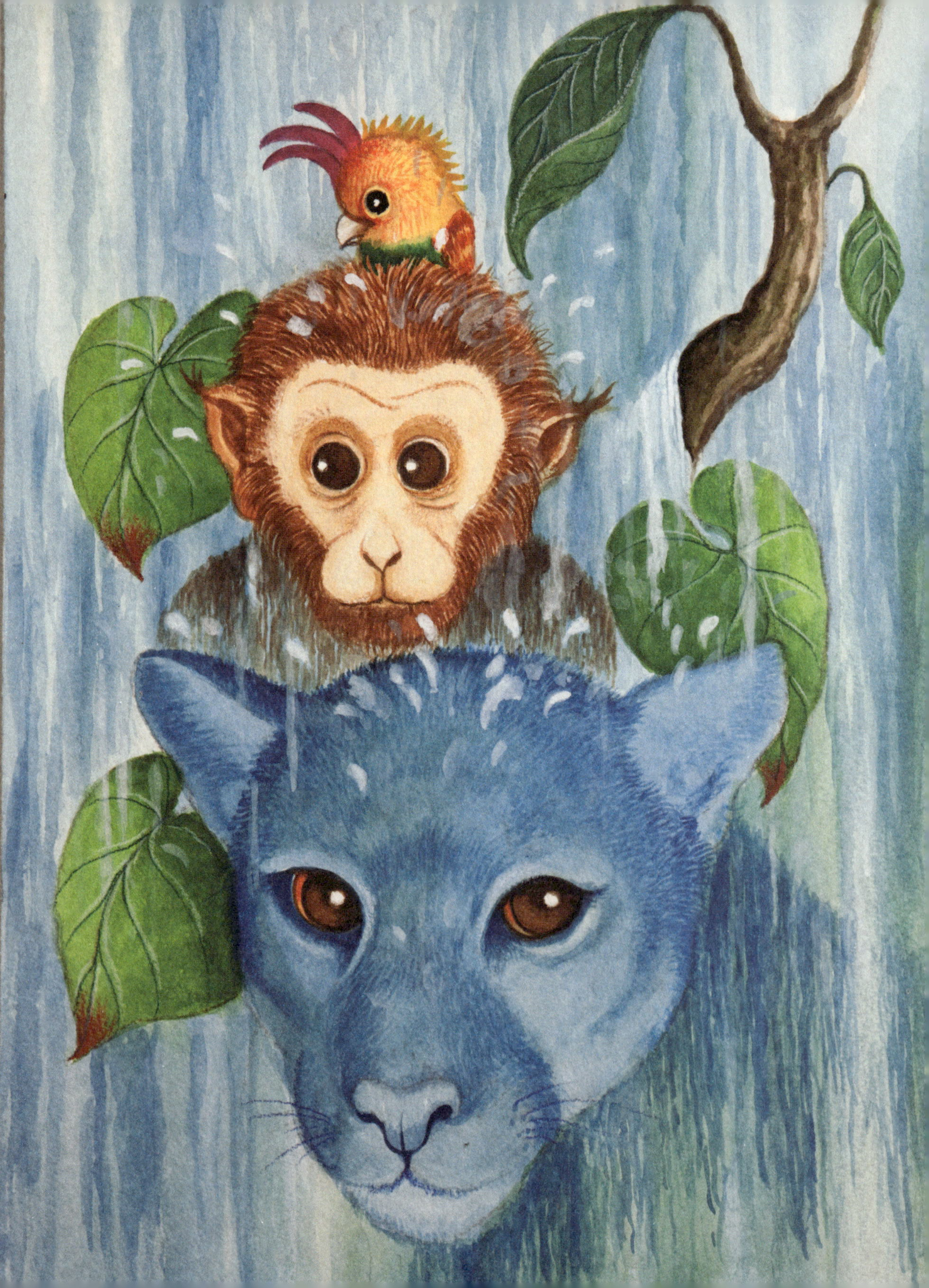

from roaring. 'The winds that carried the great birds also whirled inside me.'

'You will learn the meaning of the whirling winds,' said Grandfather Monkey. 'Now it is time to rest under the stars. There is another place you must go before you understand the call of the Wild Islands. And you will choose the time.'

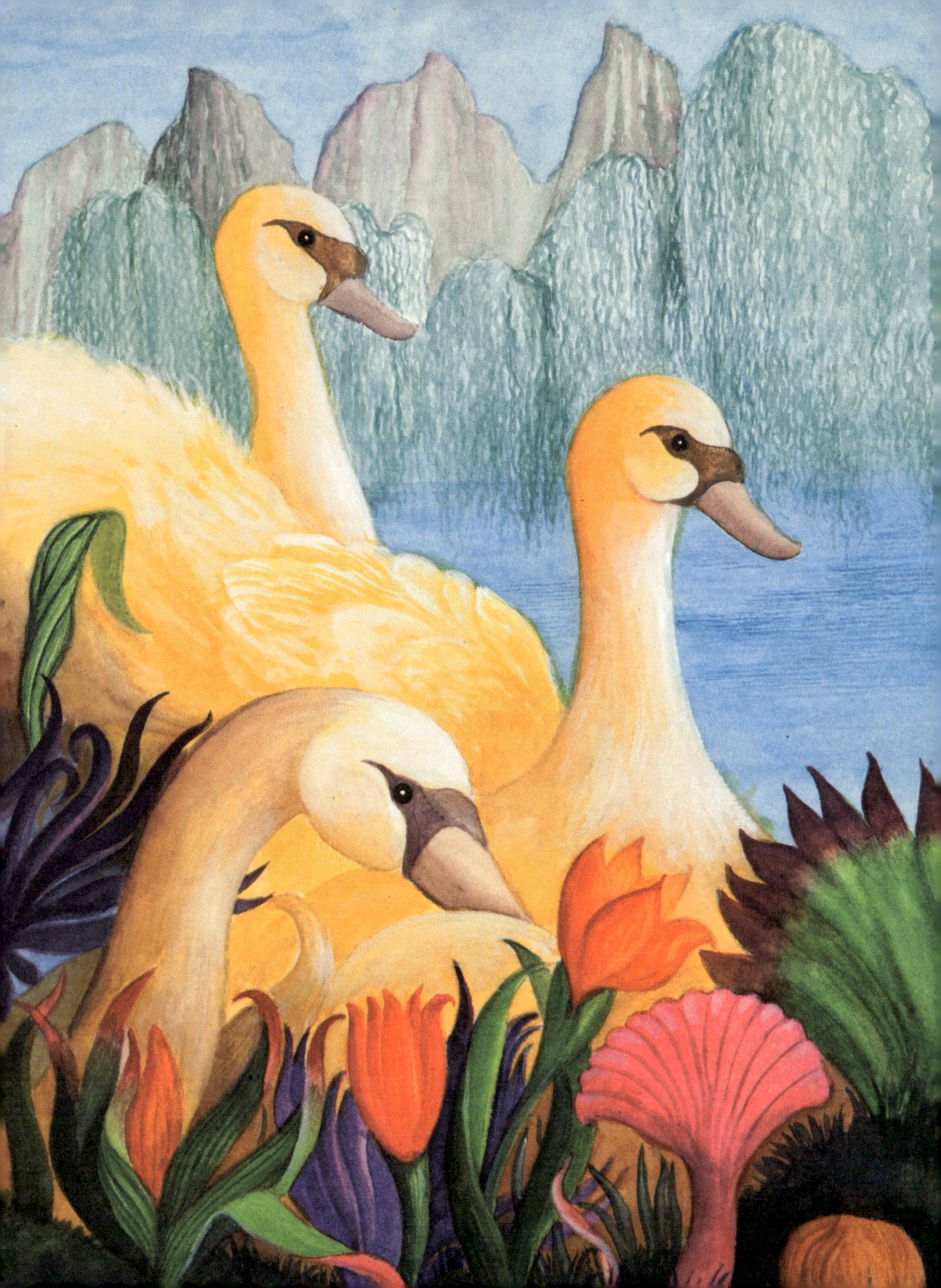

The Migrating Swans

The passing months were peaceful for Babayan. He built a hut. He planted a garden. He slept under the stars. But some nights, when the shifting winds rustled through the palms, Babayan would have strange dreams. He would wake up with a start and hear the echo of a roar that sounded like his own voice. Or his body would tremble, and he would rush to the water's edge. Sometimes, he would stare far out to sea with the Star Stone in his paws.

Then one day, while Babayan was resting by a quiet cove, a flock of migrating swans landed near him. 'Good morning,' said Babayan. Most of the swans were too shy to reply, but one strutted up to Babayan.

'I've heard of you,' he said, as he spread out his wings and began to preen. 'They say you have already learned the secrets of the Shayma Bayma Islands, even though you are new here.'

'I have travelled to all the islands,' answered Babayan modestly.

'All the islands?' questioned the swan as he arched his long neck. 'Even the Faraway Islands?'

'No. I haven't heard of them.'

'Well, you haven't seen anything until you've seen the Faraway Islands,' said the swan with a haughty turn of his head. And, with a flash of their wings, the swans were gone.

Babayan went to Grandfather Monkey. 'I have learnt of the Faraway Islands, and

I would like to go there.'

'The Faraway Islands are beautiful, but they are near the Wild Islands beyond our border,' answered Grandfather Monkey. 'Our ancestors, the Voyagers, first settled there when they left the Wild Islands to form a kingdom where beast would not prey upon beast.'

'Why didn't you tell me about the Faraway Islands before?'

'You were not ready.'

'Now I am,' said Babayan.

The Voyage

As if by an unknown signal, Grandfather Monkey summoned the birds to carry the news of Babayan's journey. It had been many generations since a member of the island kingdom had crossed the Great Sea. But the knowledge of the Voyagers had not been forgotten.

With wood from the totara tree and pitch from the sayna root, the animals of Shayma Bayma helped Babayan build a boat. The songbirds sewed dark blue sails with bright white stars and the spiderbirds wove Babayan a coat with a special pocket for his Star Stone. The flying turtles loaded the boat with food and water. Kookatu, Teema and Paw were chosen to be his crew.

When the full moon rose, the animals gathered on the beach to watch Babayan depart. As his boat passed through the island kingdom, the zebrons raised their horns, the big cats roared, and the talking Palms bowed.

For weeks, the winds carried Babayan's boat over the sea with miraculous speed. Kookatu was the lookout, Teema trimmed the sails, and Babayan and Paw took turns at the helm. In the evening, they stretched out on the deck under the stars. Teema played his flute, and they laughed and told stories until the waves lulled them to sleep. Soon they could see the Faraway Islands in the distance.

Then the air became still. The sea grew wide and empty, and they began to drift. The tides moved in one direction then another, but they never moved the boat closer to the Faraway Islands. Days passed and still they drifted.

Paw's head drooped and so did his tail. 'There are no clouds to shield us from the sun.'

Teema crouched in a patch of shade. 'And at night, the clouds are so thick we cannot read the stars.'

'Let's turn back,' said Kookatu. His throat was so dry he could not even chirp. But the wind would not let them turn back. With sudden force, it drove the boat towards the dark horizon. The sky closed in around them and the sea grew wild with waves. Babayan drew Kookatu, Teema and Paw close to him as the dark waters rushed over the boat. He struggled to find some rope and, with it, he bound them to the mast.

Babayan knew that even though he was a mighty beast, his roar was not stronger than the storm and his arms were not stronger than the sea. As the boat bowed to the darkness, Babayan reached in his pocket for the Star Stone. It glowed warm in his paw, and he remembered the words of the Queen of the Stars: 'If you are in

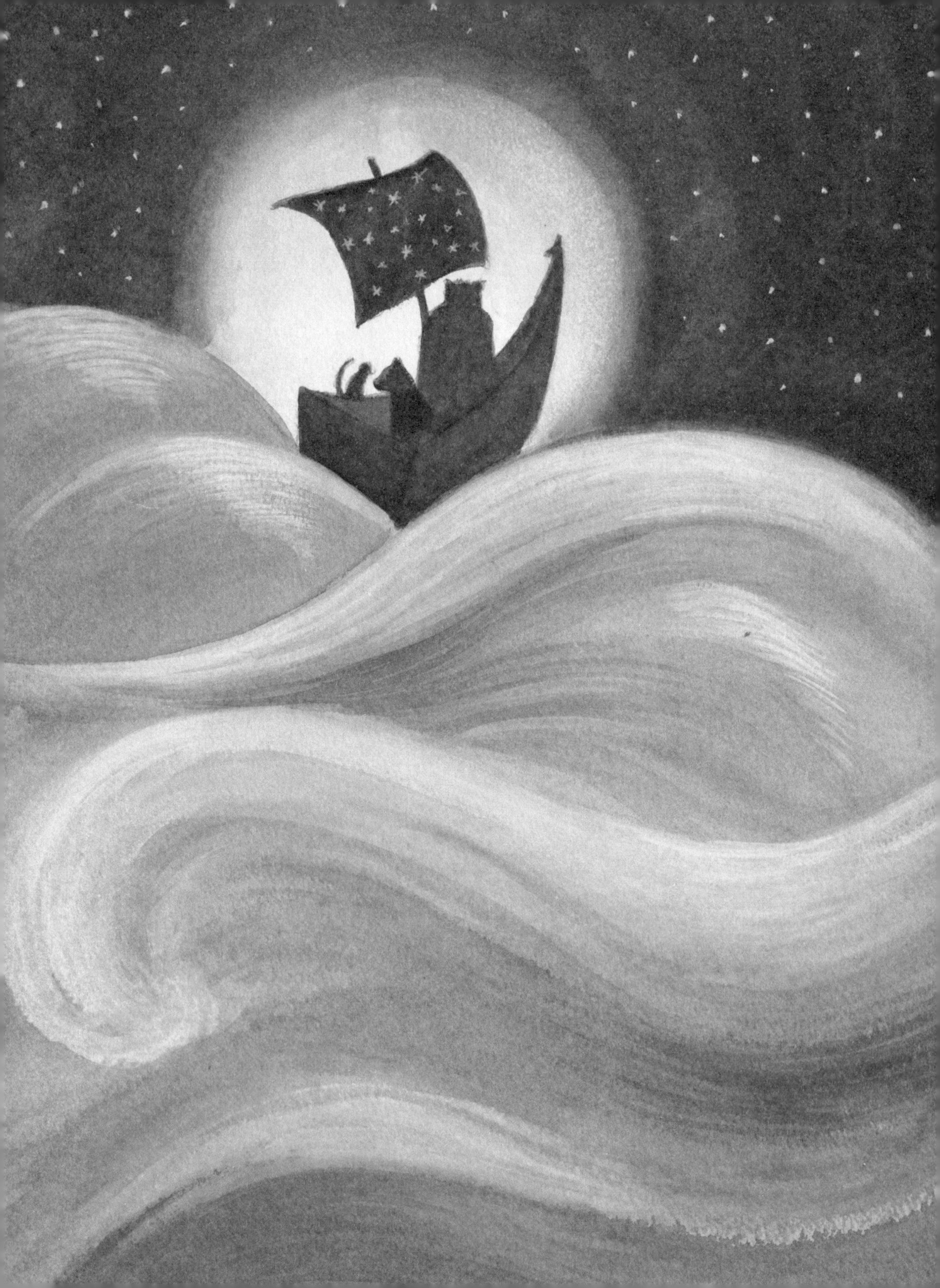

danger, I will come.' He called to her, and she answered through the wind: 'I am here.'

A circle of light formed around Babayan's boat and it sailed calmly through the raging sea to the Faraway Islands.

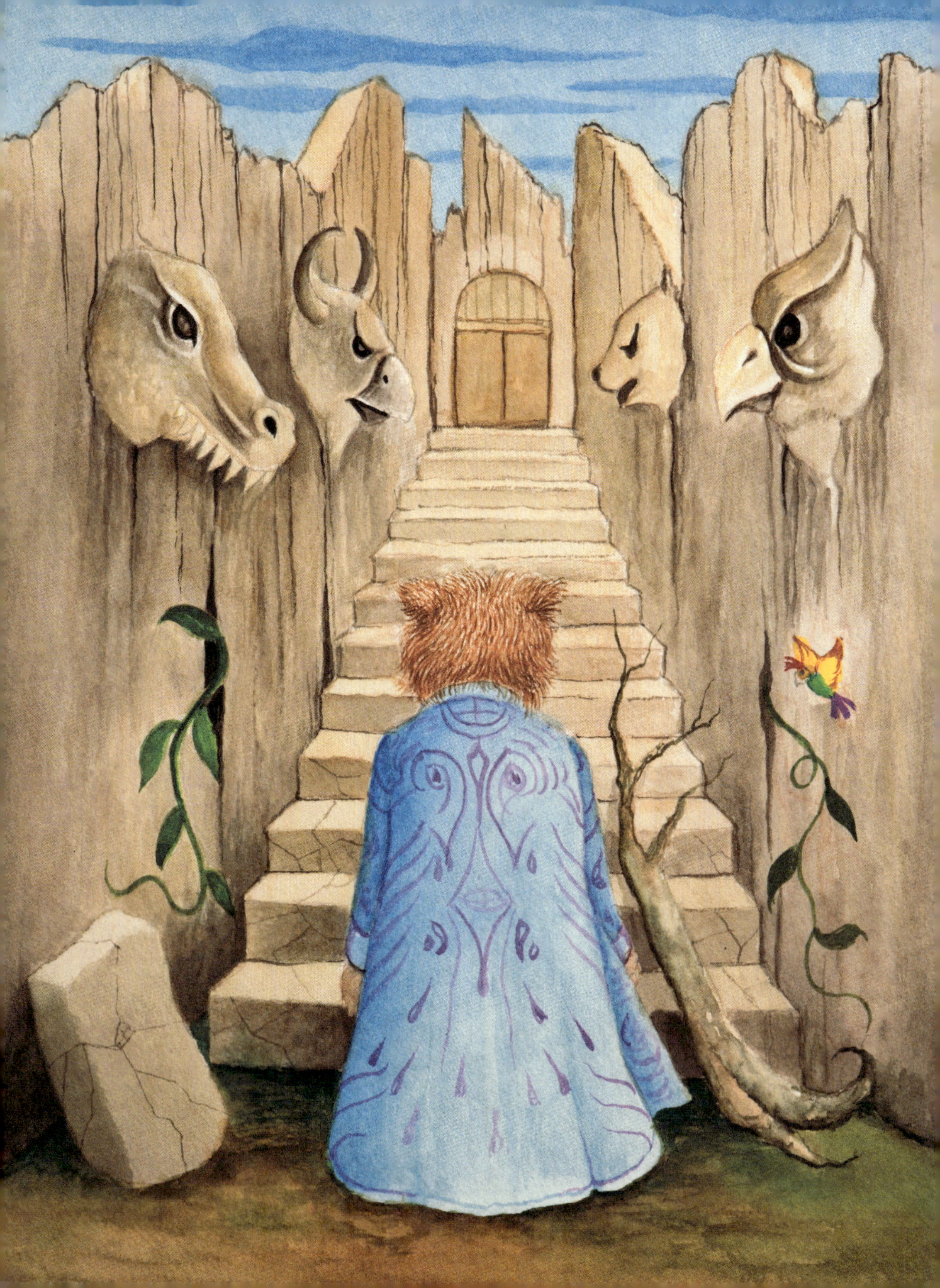

The Faraway Islands

Babayan, Kookatu, Teema and Paw awoke from an enchanted sleep in the cove of the Faraway Islands. The air was filled with the sweet scent of wild flowers and fruit. High on the hill, half-hidden by the trees and vines, stood the Fort of the Voyagers. Below, the beach was soft and white and jewelled with stones.

'Look at all this treasure,' chirped Kookatu as he swooped down and plucked a diamond starfish from the beach. Teema climbed on Paw's back, ready to explore. Then Paw's ears perked up. They heard a deep rumbling in the distance. The earth and waters trembled, and all was quiet again.

'Stay and protect the boat,' Babayan told his friends. 'I will go ashore and climb up to the Fort of the Voyagers and look at what lies beyond.'

The climb up the hill was easy for Babayan, though the way was steep. The forest was wild, green and inviting, but when he reached the top of the hill, the land was barren. The Fort of the Voyagers stood high on the cliffs overlooking the sea.

When Babayan entered the fort, it was filled with a deep silence. Great carvings of beasts stared down at him from the high walls. Paintings with inlaid shells and stones told the story of the Voyagers. There were pictures of great battles and the building of a great ship. Babayan followed the story of the Voyagers up a winding set of steps that led to the far doors facing the sea. As Babayan began to walk up the final steps, he heard a chirp behind him.

'Kookatu, what are you doing here?'

'We followed you. We just had to,' answered Kookatu as he appeared from behind a pillar with Teema and Paw by his side.

'Have you been here long?'

'As long as you have.'

Then the ground began to shake and a burst of flames shot up over the sea.

'That is the call of the volcanoes,' said Paw with a low growl. 'It awakens the creatures from the Wild Islands.'

The ground shook again. Kookatu jumped in one of Babayan's pockets and

Teema jumped in the other. Paw crouched low to the ground.

'Don't let them see you,' came a voice from the pocket. 'Those creatures never forget the dinners they've missed.'

'I am not afraid,' answered Babayan, and he climbed the final steps to the lookout post.

There before him were the Wild Islands. Giant sea serpents guarded the waters. Dragons curled their tails around the emerald hills. Great predator birds circled above the sea. The land and water teemed with creatures rushing to avoid their enemies.

Babayan looked out at the Wild Islands and a memory awakened in him.

He saw a dark cave. He felt a cold wind. He heard a mighty roar. He remembered his old hunger for sheep.

'I was a wild monster once,' he thought. 'And I am no longer.'

Babayan turned his back on the Wild Islands. They called to him no more. With his friends by his side, he walked through the Fort of the Voyagers and returned to his boat. He was ready to go home to Shayma Bayma.

A Joyful Roar

Kookatu and Teema did not come out of Babayan's pockets until the Faraway Islands were far in the distance. By then it was dusk, and the evening stars came out in the sky. The winds swept the boat across the sea. Babayan, Kookatu, Teema and Paw worked together until their boat was enveloped in the quiet of night.

Weary from the journey, Kookatu sang himself to sleep. Paw curled up near Babayan, and soon he was asleep with Teema by his side. Babayan kept the night watch. A light rain began to fall, and Babayan made a canopy of his coat to protect his sleeping friends.

The boat rocked in the water. A few stars sparkled between the clouds. Then the clouds began to part. Babayan looked up. A stairway of silver stars appeared. It extended from high in the heavens to his boat. A shining figure began to walk down the stairs. It was the Queen of the Stars.

As she drew closer, stars showered and swirled around Babayan. Then the stars swooped under the canopy and slid down Paw's back, twirled around Teema's tail and glided under Kookatu's feathers. Kookatu, Teema and Paw woke in an instant, but they did not move or speak.

The Queen of the Stars beckoned to Babayan. He walked towards her, and she rested her hand on his shoulder.

'Babayan. Babayan.'

'Here I am.'

'You fell from a star and the wildness fell from you. Now the light of your star is inside you. Your eyes cannot see it, but it is a strong light. It will guide you wherever you journey.'

Babayan felt a peacefulness in his mighty body that he had never felt before. He wanted to speak, but no words came. The sky was becoming grey with the light of dawn. The Queen of the Stars walked on to the boat. She smiled at Babayan, Kookatu, Teema and Paw, and, with a graceful bow of her head, she disappeared.

The sun rose above the sea. The winds filled the sails. Kookatu, Teema and Paw took their posts. Babayan stood at the bow. He let out a great, mighty, joyful roar. Gulls went flying and fish went diving and the morning stars sang, 'Babayan.'

Babayan and his friends followed the joyful roar all the way home.